JUV/E
M
1998   Go tell Aunt Rhody.
.G6

$13.95

DATE			

DISCARD

© THE BAKER & TAYLOR CO.

Go Tell Aunt Rhody

Go Tell Aunt Rhody

Illustrated by Aliki

Macmillan Publishing Company
New York

Macmillan Publishing Company
866 Third Avenue, New York, NY 10022
Collier Macmillan Canada, Inc.
First published 1974; reissued 1986.
Printed in the United States of America

10 9 8 7 6 5 4 3 2

The text of this book is set in Garamond Old Style.
The illustrations are painted in gouache.
Library of Congress Cataloging-in-Publication Data
Main entry under title: Go tell Aunt Rhody. 1. Children's songs.
2. Folk-songs, American. [1. Folk songs, American] I. Aliki, illus.
M1998.G   784.4'973   74-681   ISBN 0-02-700410-4

For Jolly and Alfred and their little women,
Emily, Elizabeth, Kate and Nell

Go tell Aunt Rhody,

go tell Aunt Rhody,

Go tell Aunt Rhody

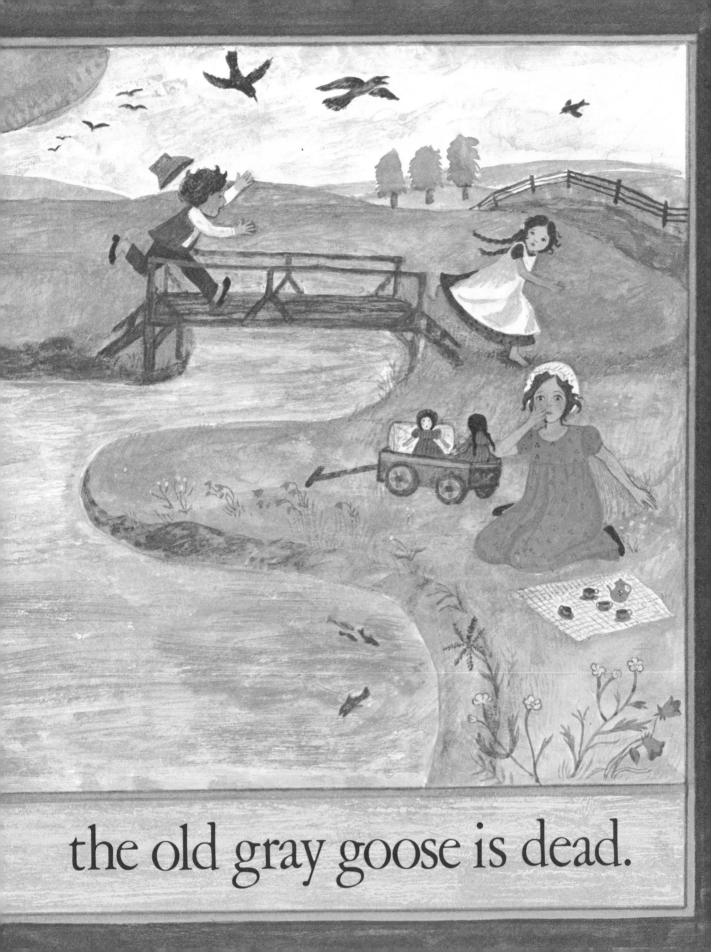

the old gray goose is dead.

The one she's been saving

to make a feather bed.

The old gander's weeping

because his wife is dead.

The goslings are mourning

because their mother's dead.

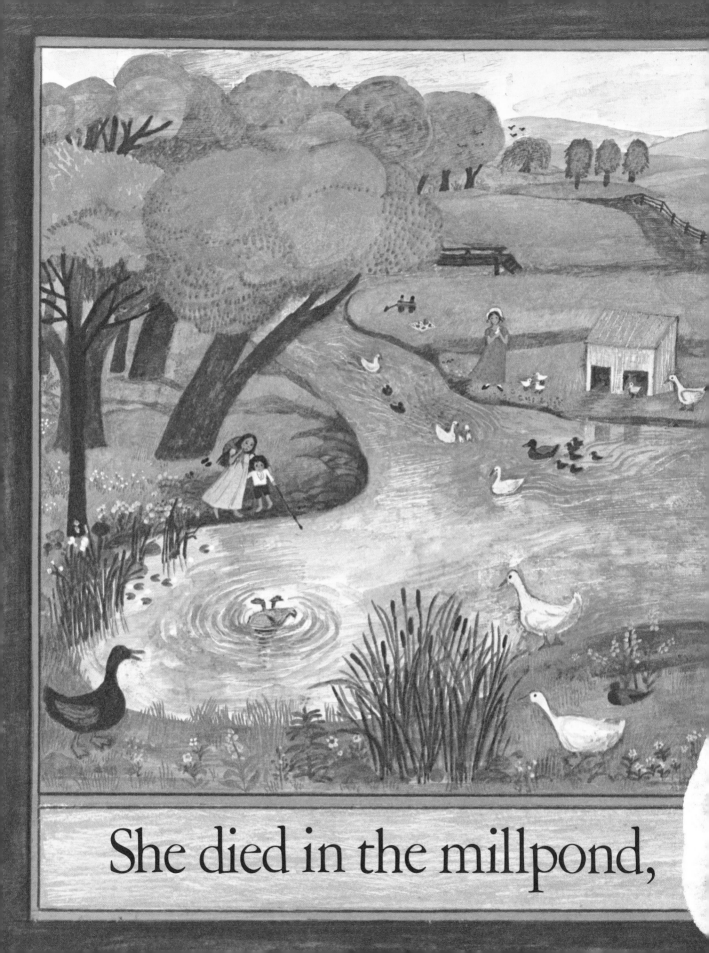

She died in the millpond,

standing on her head.

Go tell Aunt Rhody,

go tell Aunt Rhody,

Go tell Aunt Rhody

the old gray goose is dead.

Go Tell Aunt Rhody

F Major   C7

Traditional American Folk Song
Arranged by Gretchen Amussen

1. Go tell Aunt Rho - dy, _____ The
2. The one she's been sav - ing, The

Go tell Aunt Rho - dy, _____ The
one she's been sav - ing, The

Go tell Aunt Rho - dy The
one she's been sav - ing To

old gray goose is dead.
make a feath - er bed.

3. The old gander's weeping,
   The old gander's weeping,
   The old gander's weeping
   Because his wife is dead.

4. The goslings are mourning,
   The goslings are mourning,
   The goslings are mourning
   Because their mother's dead.

5. She died in the millpond,
   She died in the millpond,
   She died in the millpond,
   Standing on her head.

6. Go tell Aunt Rhody,
   Go tell Aunt Rhody,
   Go tell Aunt Rhody
   The old gray goose is dead.

"Go Tell Aunt Rhody" is a folk song that did not start out as a folk song. More than two hundred years ago a famous French writer and musician, Jean Jacques Rousseau, wrote an opera called *The Village Soothsayer*. The opera was performed in France for the king, Louis XV, and in England too. After many years, the opera was forgotten except for one melody in it. People played it on the piano, the harp and the guitar. Later the song reached the United States. Words were put to it, and one version was called "Go Tell Aunt Rhody." Over the years it has become a favorite lullaby.